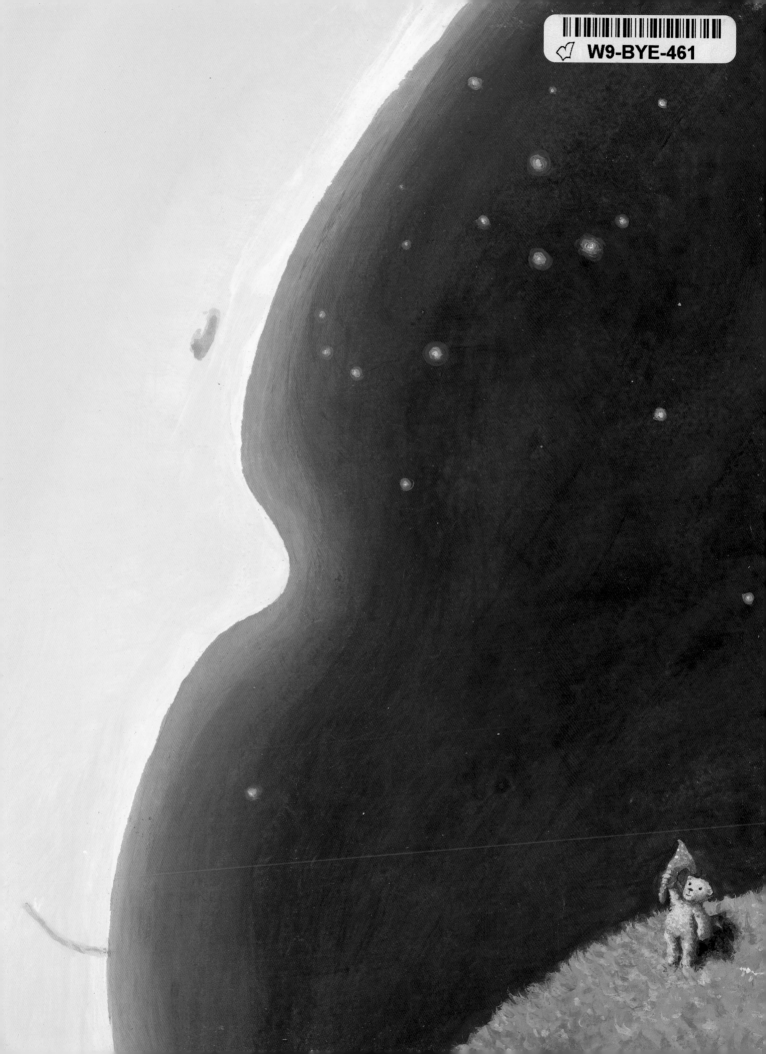

This book is based on a television
program for the German series *Seven Stones*
that appeared on the ZDF network.

© 1997 by Coppenrath Verlag, 48155 Münster, Germany.
This 2006 edition published by Backpack Books by arrangement
with Coppenrath Verlag, Germany.

Backpack Books
122 Fifth Avenue
New York, NY 10011

ISBN-13: 978-0-7607-8941-4
ISBN-10: 0-7607-8941-X

Printed and bound in China
3 5 7 9 10 8 6 4 2

Moonbeam Bear

By Rolf Fänger
and Ulrike Möltgen

Translated by Marianne Martens

Moonbeam Bear loved to watch the moon.

For seven years, he spent every evening in front of his house, watching the moon make its way across the sky. Sometimes he stayed up until long after midnight.

He knew exactly how many days it took for the moon to wax and wane and become full. He knew the moon's route across the sky— from the old barn to the hill with three trees—and he knew by heart which stars the moon would meet on its way.

The moon was his best friend.

Moonbeam Bear wished he could get closer to the moon.

Once he climbed to the top of a very tall ladder and stretched out his paw. But the moon was too far away, and Moonbeam Bear almost fell flat on his nose.

At the edge of the lake, he thought he could touch the moon, but he quickly learned that what he saw was only the reflection of the moon on the water.

Nights when there was a new moon were especially hard, because the whole world was completely dark and Moonbeam Bear missed his friend terribly.

One night, when the moon had waned and gotten very, very thin, he had an idea.

Moonbeam Bear hid in the old barn
and waited for the moon to poke
its nose over the horizon.

As soon as it did, he tossed out
a long lasso and pulled the moon
down from the night sky.

The other animals were a little surprised about the total darkness that night, but they thought it was just a new moon and went to bed early.

When the moon didn't rise on the following night they were very concerned and, by the third night, they decided to call a meeting.

"The moon has disappeared," said wise Crow. "Has anyone seen it? Does anyone have any clues?"

"Come to think of it," said Rabbit, "three nights ago I saw a bright yellow glow coming from Farmer Jones's barn. I'll bet you he stole the moon!"

"What a rat!" shouted the animals.

"If that's true," said wise Crow, "it's up to us to set the moon free."

"But it's so dark outside," whimpered Lark.

"We can light the way," said the glowworms, joining together to form a beautiful shape in the night sky.

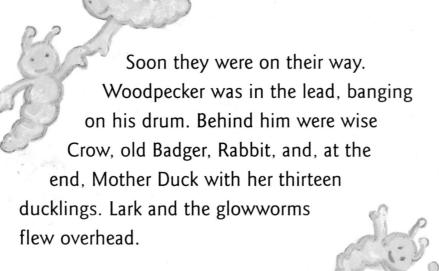

Soon they were on their way. Woodpecker was in the lead, banging on his drum. Behind him were wise Crow, old Badger, Rabbit, and, at the end, Mother Duck with her thirteen ducklings. Lark and the glowworms flew overhead.

When they arrived at Farmer Jones's house, they stood in a semicircle in front of his door. Woodpecker sounded a drum roll, and all together the animals shouted, "You are surrounded! Give back the moon immediately!"

At first nothing happened. Then they could hear Farmer Jones shuffling through the house.

"What is going on?" he asked when he opened the door.

"You stole the moon! Rabbit saw you hiding it in your barn. Admit it!"

Farmer Jones laughed. "The light Rabbit saw must have been my new flashlight. It does shine almost as brightly as the moon."

"It sure does!" said the animals, covering up their eyes.

"But if you didn't steal the moon," asked Crow, "who did?"

"I don't know," said Farmer Jones, "but I'll help you look. Follow me!"

Although Farmer Jones's new flashlight was nearly as bright as the moon, its light didn't last very long. Soon it started to flicker, and then it went out completely.

"Modern junk!" grumbled Farmer Jones, and he asked the glowworms to shine a little brighter.

They were happy to oblige. But, just as the group reached the old barn, the glowworms got very tired and fell asleep in the grass.

"What do we do now?" grumbled Farmer Jones.

"Look! Look!" shouted the ducklings, jumping up and down. "We see something bright over there."

"But little ones," said Mother Duck softly, "that's Moonbeam Bear's house. Maybe he has a new flashlight too."

"I don't think so," said Farmer Jones. "Something else is behind that light. Follow me!"

So they marched over to Moonbeam Bear's house. When they opened the door, they all gasped . . .

There was Moonbeam Bear with his arm around the moon!

The ducklings started to giggle, and soon everyone was laughing so hard that Moonbeam Bear put his finger to his lips and said, "Shhhhh! I'm trying to read the moon to sleep. If he doesn't get enough sleep, he won't shine as brightly tomorrow."

"Wait a minute," said Mother Duck. "The moon belongs in the sky where all of us can see him. You can't just keep him here."

"But it's no fun to read alone and sleep alone," said Moonbeam Bear. "The moon is my best friend. You're all welcome to come and visit us any time you like!"

"I'm sorry," said Crow, "but there are many animals and people who love the moon. Please put him back where he belongs."

Then Moonbeam Bear had a great idea.

"All right," he said, "I'll put him back, but only if once a month, when there's a new moon and it's dark anyway, the moon can come down and visit me."

"I think that's a fine idea," said Farmer Jones. All the animals nodded in agreement.

So Moonbeam Bear carried the moon back to the spot behind the three trees and carefully put him back in the night sky.

"Good-bye friend," said Moonbeam Bear softly, "I'll see you again soon."

Ever since that night, Moonbeam Bear watches his friend as he moves across the sky and carefully calculates how long it will be until the moon can come down to visit again.

Sometimes Farmer Jones comes by and Moonbeam Bear tells him all about the waning moon, the waxing moon, the stars and the planets, and all the amazing things you can see in the night sky.

Farmer Jones just loves those stories!